For Sally and Wembury Beach,
and to Peter and Margaret Bryan,
Karen, Jacqui and Alison,
with love

First United States edition 1991

Copyright © 1990 by Simon James

Margaret K. McElderry Books
Macmillan Publishing Company
866 Third Avenue
New York, NY 10022

First published by Walker Books Ltd, London
Printed in Hong Kong
10 9 8 7 6 5 4 3 2 1
Library of Congress Cataloging-in-Publication data is available upon request.
ISBN 0-689-50528-0

Sally and the Limpet

Simon James

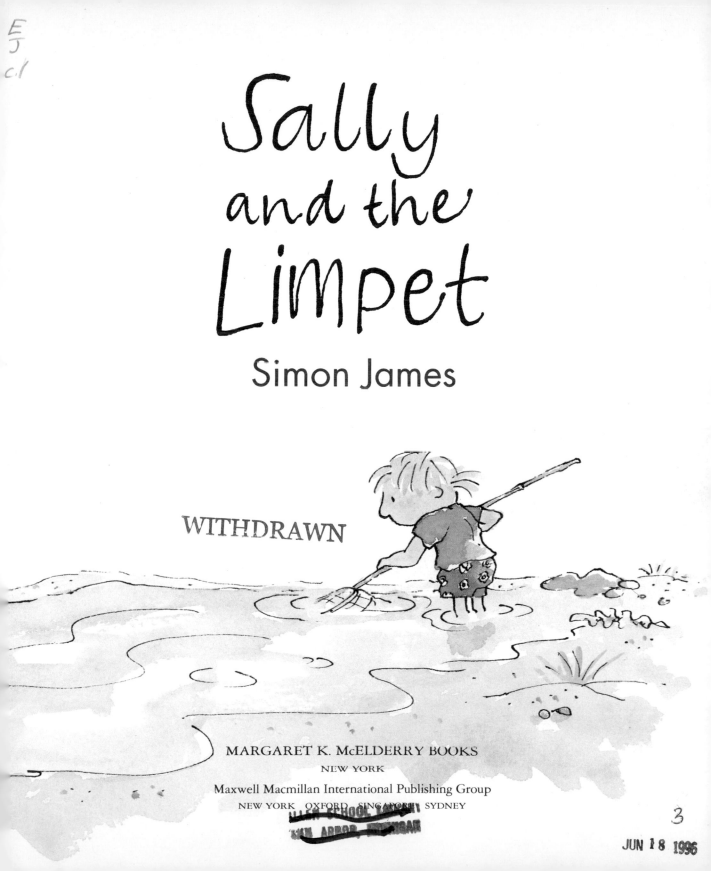

MARGARET K. McELDERRY BOOKS

NEW YORK

Maxwell Macmillan International Publishing Group

NEW YORK OXFORD SINGAPORE SYDNEY

Not long ago, on a Sunday, Sally was down on the beach exploring, when she found a

brightly colored, bigger-than-usual limpet shell.
She wanted to take it home but, as she pulled,

the limpet made a little squelching noise
and held on to the rock.

5

The harder Sally tugged, the more tightly
the limpet held on,

until, suddenly, Sally slipped and
fell – with the limpet stuck to her finger.

Though she pulled with all her might, it just wouldn't come off. So she ran over to her dad.

7

He heaved and groaned, but the limpet made a little squelching noise and held on even tighter.

So, that afternoon, Sally went home in the
car with the limpet stuck to her finger.

When they got home, her dad tried using his tools.
Her brother tried offering it lettuce and cucumber.

But, that night, Sally went to bed with
the limpet stuck to her finger.

Next day was school.

All her friends tried to pull the limpet off her finger.
Mr. Wobblyman, the nature teacher,
said that limpets
live for twenty years
and stay all their
lives on the
same rock.

In the afternoon, Sally's mother took her
to the hospital, to see the doctor.

He tried chemicals, injections, potions, and pinchers.
Sally was beginning to feel upset.

Everyone was making
too much fuss all around her.

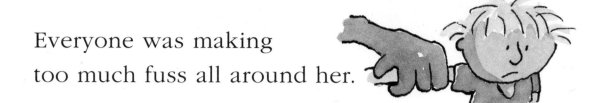

She kicked over the doctor's chair and ran.

She ran through the endless corridors.
She just wanted to be on her own.

She ran out of the hospital and through the town.

She didn't stop when she got to the beach.

She ran through people's sandcastles.
She even ran over a fat man.

When she reached the water, she jumped in
with all her clothes on.

Sally landed with a big splash

and then just sat in the water.
The limpet, feeling at home once more,

made a little squelching noise and
wiggled off her finger.

23

But Sally didn't forget what Mr. Wobblyman,
the nature teacher, had said.

Very carefully, she lifted the limpet
by the top of its shell.
She carried it back across
the beach, past the
fat man she had
walked on,

and gently, so gently, put the limpet back
on the very same rock where she had found it
the day before. Then, humming to herself,

she took the long way home across the beach.

27

28